UP THE CHIMNEY

retold by Margaret Hodges

illustrated by Amanda Harvey

Holiday House/New York

To Dorothy Dressler
M. H.

To Bill Street
A. H.

Up the Chimney is retold by Margaret Hodges from "The Old Witch"
in Joseph Jacobs's *More English Folk and Fairy Tales*. New York.
Putnam, 1904.

Text copyright © 1998 by Margaret Hodges
Illustrations copyright © 1998 by Amanda Harvey
ALL RIGHTS RESERVED
Printed in the United States of America
FIRST EDITION
Library of Congress Cataloging-in-Publication Data
Hodges, Margaret, 1911–
Up the chimney / by Margaret Hodges; illustrated by Amanda
Harvey. — 1st ed.
p.   cm.
Summary: A retelling of an English folk tale in which two sisters
who go out to seek their fortune receive very different treatment.
ISBN 0-8234-1354-3 (hardcover)
[1. Fairy tales.   2. Folklore—England.]   I. Harvey, Amanda, ill.
II. Title.
PZ8.H653Up   1998   97-34116   CIP   AC
398.2'0941'02—dc21
[E]

Once upon a time there were two girls who lived with their mother and father. The family had kept their money in a long-tailed bag, but it had been stolen and their father had no work, so the girls wanted to go away and seek their fortunes.

Now one girl wanted to find work in the town, and her mother said she might live there if she could find a job.

So she started for the town. Well, she went all about the town, but no one wanted a girl like her.

So she went on farther into the country,

and she came to a place where there was an oven with lots of bread baking. And the bread said, "Little girl, little girl, take us out, take us out. We have been baking seven years, and no one has come to take us out."

So the girl took out the bread, laid it on the ground, and went on her way.

Then she met a cow, and the cow said, "Little girl, little girl, milk me, milk me! Seven years have I been waiting, and no one has come to milk me."

The girl milked the cow into the pails that stood by.

As she was thirsty she drank some and left the rest in the pails by the cow.

Then she went on a little bit farther and came to an apple tree so loaded with fruit that its branches were breaking down, and the tree said, "Little girl, little girl, help me shake my fruit. My branches are breaking, they are so heavy."

And the girl said, "Of course I will, you poor tree."

So she shook the fruit all off,

propped up the branches, and left the fruit on the ground under
the tree.

Then she went on again till she came to a house.

Now in this house there lived a witch, and this witch took girls into her house as servants. When she heard that this girl had left her home to seek work, she said that she would try her and give her good wages.

The witch told the girl what work she was to do. "You must keep the house clean and tidy, sweep the floor and the hearth; but there is one thing you must never do. You must never look up the chimney, or something bad will happen to you."

The girl promised to do as she was told, but one morning as she was cleaning, and the witch was out, she forgot what the witch had said, and looked up the chimney. When she did this a great bag of money fell down in her lap. She could hardly believe her eyes, so she looked carefully.

"I know this bag," she said. "It belongs to my father and mother."

She started to go off home with it,

but when she had gone some way she heard the witch coming after her.

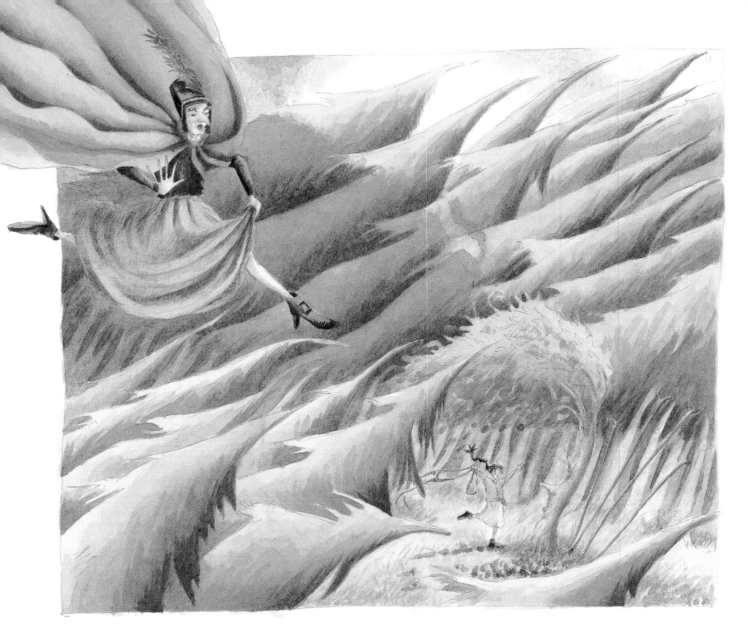

So she ran to the apple tree and cried:

> *Apple tree, apple tree, hide me,*
> *So the old witch can't find me;*
> *If she does, she'll pick my bones,*
> *And bury me under the marble stones.*

So the apple tree hid her.

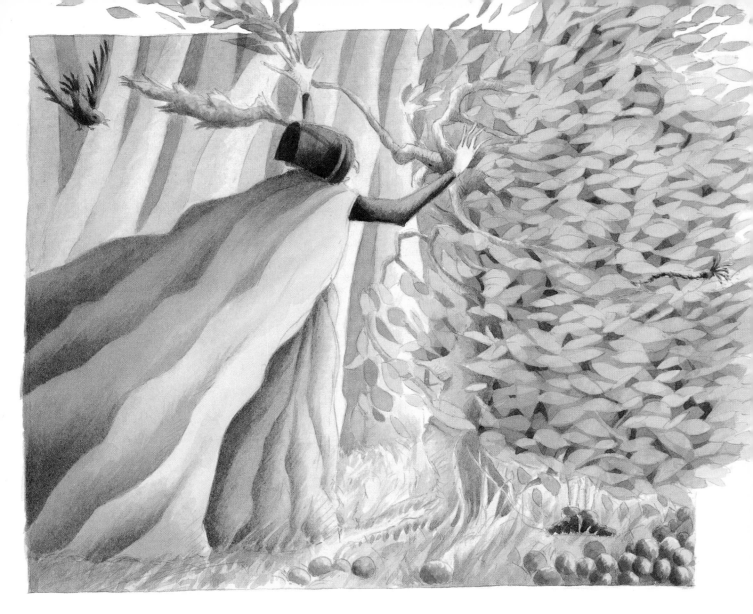

When the witch came to the tree, she said:

> *Tree of mine, tree of mine,*
> *Have you seen a girl*
> *With a willy-willy wag, and a long-tailed bag,*
> *Who's stole my money, all I had?*

And the apple tree said, "No, mother, not for seven years."
When the witch had gone on another way, the girl ran off again.

Just as she got to the cow, she heard the witch coming after her again, so she ran to the cow and cried:

> *Cow, cow, hide me,*
> *So the old witch can't find me;*
> *If she does, she'll pick my bones,*
> *And bury me under the marble stones.*

So the cow hid her.

When the old witch came up, she looked about and said to the cow:

> *Cow of mine, cow of mine,*
> *Have you seen a girl*
> *With a willy-willy wag, and a long-tailed bag,*
> *Who's stole my money, all I had?*

And the cow said, "No, mother, not for seven years."

When the witch had gone off another way, the girl went on again, and when she was near the oven she heard the witch coming after her again, so she ran to the oven and cried:

> *Oven, oven, hide me,*
> *So the old witch can't find me;*
> *If she does, she'll break my bones,*
> *And bury me under the marble stones.*

And the oven said, "I've no room, ask the baker." And the baker hid her behind the oven.

When the witch came up, she looked here and there and every-
where, and then said to the baker:

> *Man of mine, man of mine,*
> *Have you seen a girl*
> *With a willy-willy wag, and a long-tailed bag,*
> *Who's stole my money, all I had?*

So the baker said, "Look in the oven." The old witch went to look,
and the oven said, "Get in and look in the furthest corner."
The witch got into the oven, and when she was inside, he shut the
door, and there she stayed for a very long time.

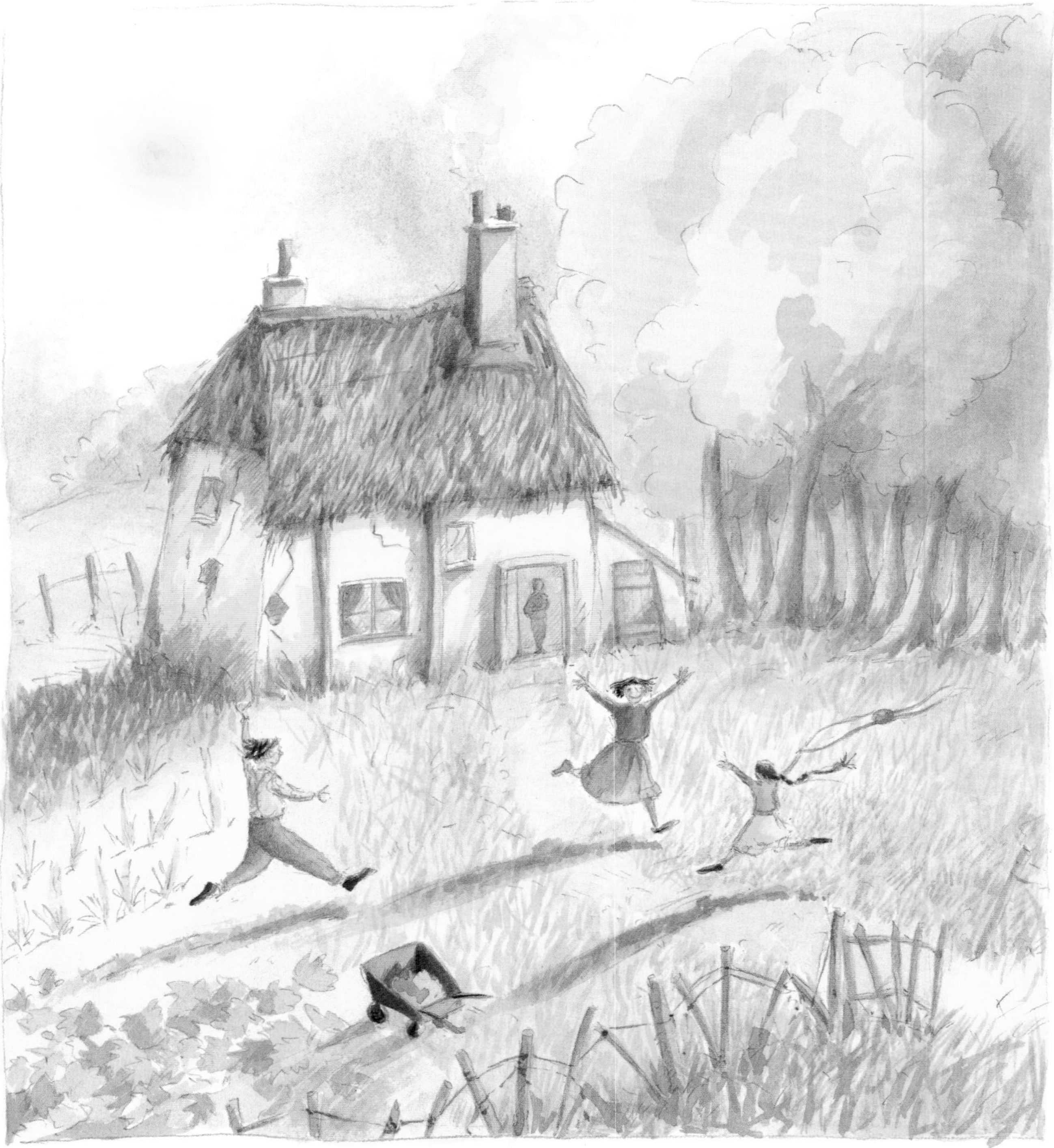

The girl went off again, and reached her home with the money bag that the witch had stolen.

She gave the long-tailed bag to her mother and father, and she married a good man and lived happily ever after.

Well, the other sister thought she would go and do the same.

She went the same way. But when she reached the oven, the bread said, "Little girl, little girl, take us out. Seven years have we been baking, and no one has come to take us out."

But the girl said, "No, I don't want to burn my fingers."

So she went on till she met the cow, and the cow said, "Little girl, little girl, milk me, milk me, do. Seven years have I been waiting, and no one has come to milk me."

But the girl said, "No, I can't milk you. I'm in a hurry," and went on faster.

Then she came to the apple tree, and the apple tree asked her to help shake the fruit.

"No, I can't," she said. "Another day perhaps I may,"

and went on till she came to the witch's house.

Well, it happened to her just the same as to the other girl. One day when the witch was out, she forgot what she was told, looked up the chimney, and down fell a bag of money. Well, she thought she would be off at once.

When she reached the apple tree, she heard the witch coming after her, and she cried:

Apple tree, apple tree, hide me,
So the old witch can't find me;
If she does, she'll break my bones,
And bury me under the marble stones.

But the tree didn't answer, and she ran on further. Presently the witch came up and said:

Tree of mine, tree of mine,
Have you seen a girl
With a willy-willy wag, and a long-tailed bag,
Who's stole my money, all I had?

The tree said, "Yes, mother, she's gone down that way."

So the old witch went after her and caught her. She took all the
money away from her, beat her with a broomstick, and sent her off
home just as she was.